BUSTED!

Tyndale House books by Tim LaHaye and Jerry B. Jenkins

The Left Behind series
Left Behind
Tribulation Force
Nicolae
Soul Harvest
Apollyon
Assassins
The Indwelling—available spring 2000

Left Behind: The Kids
#1: The Vanishings
#2: Second Chance
#3: Through the Flames
#4: Facing the Future
#5: Nicolae High
#6: The Underground
#7: Busted!
#8: Death Strike

Tyndale House books by Tim LaHaye
Are We Living in the End Times?
How to Be Happy though Married
Spirit-Controlled Temperament
Transformed Temperaments
Why You Act the Way You Do

Tyndale House books by Jerry Jenkins
And Then Came You
As You Leave Home
Still the One

Busted!

LEFT BEHIND™

>THE KIDS<

Jerry B. Jenkins

Tim LaHaye

WITH CHRIS FABRY

TYNDALE
KIDS

TYNDALE HOUSE PUBLISHERS, INC.
WHEATON, ILLINOIS

Visit Tyndale's exciting Web site at www.tyndale.com

Discover the latest Left Behind news at www.leftbehind.com

Published in association with the literary agency of Alive
Communications, Inc., 1465 Kelly Johnson Blvd., Suite 320, Colorado
Springs, CO 80920.

Designed by Jenny Destree

ISBN 0-8423-4327-X

Printed in the United States of America

06 05 04 03 02 01 00
 9   8   7   6   5   4   3   2   1

To Megan

TABLE OF CONTENTS

What's Gone On Before

THE underground newspaper had been Vicki Byrne's idea. Judd Thompson caught the vision and created it, along with Ryan, Lionel, and two new friends. The Young Tribulation Force wanted everyone in school to know the truth: Jesus Christ had taken true Christians away in the Rapture. The kids risked everything to get that paper inside Nicolae Carpathia High School.

Vicki was caught and questioned by school authorities. Finally, the principal, Mrs. Jenness, said, "We're going to let you think about it overnight, Vicki. Your future depends on what you tell us. Tomorrow we want you back here with your parents."

Vicki wondered if her mom and dad would be proud of what she was doing. Could they see her? That thought overwhelmed her, and she began to cry.

"It's OK, Vicki," Mrs. Jenness said, handing her a tissue. "You have a talk with your family. I'm sure they'll want you to do the right thing."

For the first time since she had met her new friends, she felt utterly alone.

ONE

On the Run

SOMEONE was following her in a car. Vicki clutched her books to her chest and walked toward town. She didn't look back. She couldn't risk letting them know she suspected.

Mrs. Jenness had let her go. That was a surprise. But Vicki would have stayed all night without ratting on her friends. But would her friends be as faithful to her?

Seeing Shelly and her mother in the principal's office had sickened Vicki. Shelly had been sincere about her faith, hadn't she? Could it have been an act? The sight of Judd, John, and Mark turning away from her down the hall made her heart sink. Didn't they care? Or were they trying to protect her by keeping their distance?

Vicki had a good idea who was following her: someone from school assigned to see where she went. Perhaps Judd and the others had figured that out. They wouldn't have simply abandoned her.

Vicki had to get back to her friends. She had to talk with Pastor Bruce. When Mrs. Jenness discovered she had no parents, all the kids would be at risk. She needed to keep moving and stay away from Judd's house.

Vicki looked in shop windows and followed the reflection of the trailing car. When it stopped, she ducked into a drugstore. She sat at a bench in the back and tapped out a message on the tiny digital system on her wrist that looked like a watch. She asked Judd to meet her at a nearby park. She would try to shake whoever was following her and meet him there.

The front door opened. A man's voice. Loud. "Did a girl with red hair come in here?"

Vicki crouched beneath the prescription window.

"Right there," the cashier said.

Vicki looked up. The overhead mirror ran the length of the wall and angled down. The man behind the counter pointed toward her. Vicki remembered how her little sister, Jeanni, used to play hide-and-seek by sticking her head in the closet, her rear sticking out of the coats.

"Duh," Vicki said as she leapt to her feet.

"Stop!" the cashier shouted.

Vicki pushed open a door that said EMPLOYEES ONLY.

"Hey, you can't go in there!" the pharmacist barked.

"We'll get her," someone shouted.

Vicki locked the door behind her. Footsteps and shouts outside. Darkness inside. Vicki fumbled for a light switch. Keys were jangling, getting closer.

"What did she take?" someone said.

Vicki moved toward a thin strip of light on the other side of the room. The back door! She tripped over a chair and banged her head. The doorknob jiggled behind her.

She leaned against the back door, and it swung open to blistering light. A siren rang just above her head. She staggered out. As the door swept shut she read, "Emergency Exit Only—Alarm Will Sound."

She ran.

Judd had waited in his car after school, hoping Vicki would walk that way. After twenty minutes he was about to leave for Lionel and Ryan's school when his wrist messenger vibrated and he saw Vicki's message. He quickly sent another to Lionel and Ryan:

"Get home and keep watch. I'll be there as fast as I can."

The park had been a late-night teen hang-out. With the rise in crime, a lot of kids were afraid to go there. Judd sat in the parking lot looking at the empty swing sets. Before the disappearances, the place would have been full of little kids. Now there were no families at picnic tables or moms and dads with strollers. It was a ghost town.

"Get the car," the loud man said. "I'll meet you at the end of the alley."

Vicki heard shuffling and then silence. She didn't want to rise up from her hiding place, but the smell was overpowering. She peeked from under the lid of the huge garbage bin. No one. Something furry moved behind her. She bolted.

Vicki ran down the alley. She was halfway to the main street when a car passed. A second later it was back.

"There she is!" a man said, but she didn't see his face. She was running the other way. The alley fence was way over her head—no time to climb. Every door she tried was locked. The car pulled behind her and gunned the engine.

Judd had been so focused on getting to the park and alerting Ryan and Lionel that he forgot to let Vicki know he was waiting.

He backtracked, slowing to look in shop windows and down alleys. He heard the screech of tires and swerved to miss an oncoming car barreling around a corner. He drove past the drugstore and hung a left. Judd sped past an alley and slammed on his brakes. Vicki ran toward him, the car bearing down on her.

Judd made a U-turn and opened the passenger door. Vicki jumped in. "Go, go, go!" she shouted.

"I don't mean to be rude," Judd said, speeding away, "but you look awful."

"Thanks," Vicki said, panting. "Just get me out of here!"

Judd sped through a yellow light. The car behind had a red, but it ran through the light, swerved to miss oncoming traffic, and kept gaining.

"Who is that?" Judd said.

"It's gotta be Handlesman or somebody he told to follow me. They want us bad."

Judd turned at the next light, then into an alley. They careened around another corner and through an empty parking lot.

"Hang on," Judd said as he crossed a patch of grass and turned into a tree-lined subdivision. He flew across a bridge, spun in the entrance to a park, and came to a halt behind some shrubs. The trailing car was nowhere in sight.

"Better stay here awhile just to make sure," Judd said. "Who gave you the shiner?"

"A filing cabinet, I think," Vicki said.

Through gasps, Vicki told Judd about her interrogation at school. Judd told her they had listened to Shelly and her mother through the bug in Mrs. Jenness's office.

"What did Shelly say?" Vicki asked. "How much were you able to hear?"

"We heard Shelly crying and her mother yelling at her to give you up," he said. "Not much more."

"Then maybe they pushed her into it," Vicki said. "At least that's what I hope."

Judd sniffed. "Is it me, or is there an odor in here?"

Vicki blushed. "I hid in a garbage bin."

Judd pulled a blackened piece of banana peel from her hair. "Pretty resourceful."

"And gross," Vicki said, shuddering and rubbing her arms. "I hate goose bumps."

"Are you cold?"

She shook her head. "Judd, they told me to bring my parents tomorrow."

"They don't know about your mom and dad?"

"If they do, they're not letting on."

Judd paused. "Uh, I want to thank you. We couldn't hear the interrogation, but we could tell you handled yourself well. We were all impressed."

"You would have done the same for me."

"Mark wanted to rescue you. Said we should give ourselves up."

"He didn't think I could handle the pressure?"

"He didn't think it was fair to put you through it."

"I could've choked Handlesman," Vicki said. "He treated me like some dumb little girl, like I'd never have the brains to put two sentences together, let alone a newspaper."

"Don't worry," Judd said. "You'll get your chance to show him Monday morning."

"You're not going through with it again, are you?"

Judd nodded. "Why not? If Bruce is right, the treaty between Israel and Carpathia will be headlined around the world. We can't pass this up. We have to tell people what's ahead."

"Bruce says the treaty signals the beginning of the Tribulation, right?"

"Exactly," Judd said.

"But how are you gonna get the *Underground* inside? You've got the guard checkpoint, cameras, and every teacher in the school on the lookout."

Judd shrugged. "We've got God on our side."

Vicki ran through all her options, and none seemed very good. Judd waited until dusk to start the car.

"Can we stop and see Bruce on the way home?" Vicki said. "I want to see what he thinks."

"He could pretend to be your father," Judd said.

"That'd be lying," Vicki said. "He'd never do that."

A few cars lined the New Hope Village Church parking lot. *Maybe the Tribulation Force is meeting,* Judd thought. He parked in front and kept the engine running. He waited while Vicki dashed inside. He flipped to a news station on the radio.

"Not a day has passed without some major development with new UN Secretary-General Nicolae Carpathia," the reporter said. "And today was no exception. Cincinnati Archbishop Peter Cardinal Mathews, who some see as successor to the vanished pope, announced a new cooperative religion that would incorporate the tenets of all major religions. He calls it the Global Community Faith."

"Our religions have caused much division and bloodshed," Cardinal Mathews droned. "From this day forward we will unite under the banner of the Global Community Faith. Our logo will contain sacred symbols from religions that represent all, and from here on will encompass all. Whether we believe God is a real person or merely a concept, God is in all and above all and around all. God is in us. God is us. We are God."

Judd shook his head. What a pack of lies.

"We will elect a pope," Mathews said. "And we expect that other major religions will continue to appoint leaders in their usual cycles. But these leaders will serve the Global Community Faith and be expected to maintain the loyalty and devotion of their parishioners to the larger cause."

The reporter continued. "United Nations Secretary-General Nicolae Carpathia said the move toward one religion is a welcome change."

"'We clearly are at the most momentous juncture in world history,'" Carpathia said. "'With the consolidation to one form of currency, with the cooperation and toleration of many religions into one, with worldwide disarmament and commitment to peace, the world is truly becoming one.'"

"Another incredible development came when Nicolae Carpathia answered questions regarding the rebuilding of the Jewish temple and the future of the Islamic Dome of—"

Vicki jumped in the car and slapped the radio off.

"Go!" she shouted.

"What's going on?"

"Look," Vicki pointed.

Running toward them was an angry Coach Handlesman. Judd sped away.

"What's he doing here?" Judd said.

"Bruce's office door was kinda open, so I knocked. All of a sudden Coach Handlesman starts yelling! He accuses Bruce of crimes, says he'll have him thrown in jail. I was outta there."

"How could Coach Handlesman know about Bruce?"

Vicki shook her head. "Maybe Shelly gave them his name. Bruce went with me to her house."

"Great," Judd said. "I didn't want to drag Bruce into the middle of all this."

Judd parked near his house and watched for Coach Handlesman. When he was sure they had eluded him, Judd pulled inside the garage and lowered the door.

Lionel and Ryan peppered them with questions until late.

"No lights tonight," Judd told them. And the four would take turns watching the street.

TWO

Grilled Vicki

It WAS midnight and Judd couldn't sleep. He sat in the dark living room with his four friends. Ryan and his dog, Phoenix, kept watch at the window.

"What should we do?" Lionel said, as if the problem were as much his as Vicki's.

"We could hide her," Ryan said. "I know a bunch of places they'll never find you, Vick."

"Get your stuff and let's get outta here," Judd said. "You can stay at a motel. Anywhere. We'll find a place for you, and when things calm down, you can come back."

"You know it's not that easy," Vicki said. "You gotta face your troubles. Running only postpones things."

"Just give us until Monday when the next edition of the *Underground* comes out," Judd said. "They'll think maybe you weren't involved in the first place."

"Yeah, then they'll believe I'm the ignorant stooge Coach Handlesman thinks I am."

Judd dialed Bruce's office. No answer. The next morning, with Ryan and Phoenix asleep by the window, he tried Bruce's home. No answer.

"I don't like this," Judd said. He was startled to hear a voice answer him.

"You're gonna like *this* even less," Lionel said. "Handlesman just pulled in."

Judd called downstairs to Vicki's room as the doorbell rang. He let Handlesman wait a moment while Lionel and Ryan hid in the den. Handlesman rang again and pounded on the door. "Come on, open up. I know you're in there!"

"Mr. Handlesman, what a nice surprise," Judd said. The coach walked in and looked around the house. Phoenix growled and barked from the den.

"Is she in there?" Coach Handlesman said.

"No, I don't think that's her bark," Judd said.

"Don't get smart with me, kid. Tell me—"

"I'm right here," Vicki said. "What's the matter? Didn't think I'd show up?"

"I'm not taking the chance."

Mr. Handlesman grabbed her arm and forced her through the door.

"Where are you taking her?" Judd shouted, but Mr. Handlesman kept going.

Lionel and Ryan came out as the car pulled away.

"We're cooked," Judd said. "It's only a matter of time until they get the rest of us."

They called it a hearing, but to Vicki it felt like a trial. Mrs. Jenness, Coach Handlesman, and Mrs. Waltonen testified against her. Vicki had admitted tripping a fire alarm, and they believed she had broken into the school and distributed the *Underground*.

Candace Goodwin of Global Community Social Services scribbled on a yellow legal pad. She was a tall, thin woman with glasses. She rarely looked up from her notes and made no eye contact with Vicki until the testimony against her was over.

"I'm in charge of custodial care," Mrs. Goodwin said. "Since there's no one with you, I'll assume you lost your parents and brother and sister in the vanishings."

"That's right."

"Do you have *any* aunts, uncles, or cousins?"

"Not that I know of," Vicki said. "I tried to get in touch with a friend of my brother's in Michigan, but he's gone, too."

"Where have you been living?"

"With friends."

"Are these the friends who published the *Underground?*"

Vicki looked at Coach Handlesman. "I'm from a trailer park. What would I know about that kind of thing?"

John and Mark joined Judd, Ryan, and Lionel at the house. The next issue of the *Underground* would be the most timely.

"Bingo!" John said, as he looked at the computer screen. "The big block against rebuilding the Jewish temple is the Islamic Dome of the Rock. Both the Jews and followers of Islam claim the site as a holy place. Carpathia says he's worked out an agreement to move the Dome to New Babylon."

"That means the Jews can rebuild the temple on the original site," Ryan said, "just like it says in the Bible."

Judd tapped the keyboard and stared out

the window. "Where do you think they took her?"

"You didn't hear a word," John said.

"Yes, I did," Judd said. "I just—"

"Your mind's somewhere else," Mark interrupted. "Why don't we just stop and go look for Vicki?"

"We have to get this done," John said. "It may be our last issue anyway."

"Why don't we hide?" Mark said. "We can move everything to our house."

"Might not be a bad idea," Judd said.

"We could split up," Lionel said. "A couple of us go look for Vicki and the rest stay here."

"Vicki will get in touch if she needs us," John said.

"Wrong," Ryan said, holding up her wrist messenger. "We won't be hearing from her at all. She didn't have time to put it on."

"We have to find her then," Judd said. "I'll take Ryan, and you guys stay here."

Vicki was well into her story. She told how her parents had become Christians, what a change it had made in them, and how she felt when she was left behind.

Though she didn't use names, she told of

the tape she had seen of a pastor who predicted exactly what had happened and told how to have a relationship with God.

"He said we are all sinners, that we deserve God's judgment, but that Jesus offers us forgiveness."

Mrs. Waltonen hung her head. At first she had been interested in Vicki's story. Mrs. Waltonen had lost a grandchild and other family members. Vicki wanted to give her hope, but now she seemed closed.

"Candace, I don't think we really need to hear this, do we?" Mrs. Jenness said.

"It's good to know motivation," Mrs. Goodwin said.

Mrs. Jenness tried to look concerned. "We're here to help you, Vicki. That's what we've tried to do all along. If you won't let us, you'll face the consequences."

"Which are . . . ?"

"Two options," Mrs. Goodwin said. "An emergency shelter called The Haven. You attend the same school, and your life stays pretty normal. Spartan, but comfortable."

"And option two?"

Mrs. Goodwin shrugged. "NDC."

"Northside?" Vicki said. "The detention center?"

Coach Handlesman nodded. "Not a nice place."

Judd and Ryan passed the school parking lot. Phoenix sat in the back and chewed on a toy. Coach Handlesman's car was there, but Vicki could have been anywhere.

"Can't we get in and listen on that bug you guys planted?" Ryan said.

"Too risky. Besides, only John has keys to that room."

Judd parked on a side street, and they left Phoenix in the car. He and Ryan went straight to the administrative wing, but the windows were high and dark. They crept a little ways along the brick wall, gingerly crunching the gravel underfoot.

"Get on my shoulders," Judd said.

Ryan pulled himself up and stretched to see inside. "Next room," he said. "Move down."

"Keep your head low," Judd said as he sneaked a few yards farther.

"It's her," Ryan whispered. "There's that coach guy and two women."

A van pulled in with NDC painted on the side. Judd dropped Ryan and dove to the

19

ground. They lay there as a stocky woman climbed out.

"Looks like a dogcatcher's van," Ryan said. "There's a cage between the driver and the back seat."

"This might be our last chance," Judd said. "We have to get Vicki's wrist messenger to her."

"You've left us no choice, Vicki," Candace Goodwin said. "NDC is not our first choice, and I'm sure it's not yours."

"Listen, deary," the stocky woman drawled, "the kids we're talkin' about will eat you for lunch. You won't last a day. We try to keep control, but it's tough. Just tell these people what they want to know. No one will think less of you for it."

"This is your last chance, Vicki," Mrs. Goodwin said. "Tell us who you were working with on the newspaper, and we'll take you to The Haven."

Vicki hated the thought of the detention center. But she hated giving up her friends even worse. She would not give in. Suddenly from the hall came footsteps, then a loud knock. Ryan burst in.

"Hey, have any of you seen my dog?"

"Young man, get out of this building!"
Coach Handlesman said, standing. "You're
not allowed in here—"

"Whoa, there he is now," Ryan said.
Phoenix came bounding in, sliding past
Ryan, tripping Coach Handlesman and
making him stagger. Vicki laughed. Even
Mrs. Waltonen smiled. Coach Handlesman
started toward Ryan, who said, "Sorry!
We're goin'."

Ryan had slipped Vicki's wrist gadget to
her in the confusion. She slid it into her
pocket as Candace Goodwin was filling out a
form. "By the authority of Global Community Social Services, I give you over to the
Northside Detention Center for a period to
be determined by authorities there. I'm sorry
about this, Vicki. You seem like a genuinely
nice young lady."

Judd and Ryan watched from their car as
Vicki was put in the back of the van.

"Are we gonna follow her?" Ryan said.

"We know where she's going. Let's send
her a message."

He quickly tapped a few words and
pressed the Send button. Phoenix barked.
Someone was standing by their car. Coach

Handlesman motioned for Judd to roll down his window.

"Go home now," he said. "The excitement's over."

Vicki scrunched down in the seat so Mrs. Weems couldn't see her. She held her wrist messenger like it was gold. This was her only link with her friends. A message scrolled across the screen: "We're with you, Vicki."

She looked at the words again and again until she saw the huge chain-link fence with razor wire at the top. A splintered sign read Northside Detention Center.

The guard at the gate wore a gun.

THREE

The Lions' Den

JUDD brought everybody up to date when he got home, and he brought up the subject of finding a new place to live, now that Handlesman was onto them.

Mark gave Judd an article he had written for the *Underground* from material by Dr. Marc Feinberg, the rabbi working on the new temple. "It explains why the temple is so important."

"Great," Judd said, sitting to read it.

It's important to understand the history of the Jewish temple. King David wanted to build it, but God felt David was too much of a warrior, so he let David's son Solomon complete it. Solomon's temple was magnificent. God's people would worship God there in Jerusalem. The glory of God appeared in the temple, and it became a symbol of the hand of God protecting the nation. The people felt so secure that even when they turned from God, they believed Jerusalem was impregnable, as long as the temple stood.

The temple and the city of Jerusalem were destroyed by King Nebuchadnezzar in 587 B.C. Seventy years later a decree was given to rebuild the city and eventually the temple. That temple served Israel until it was desecrated by Antiochus Epiphanes, a Greco-Roman ruler.

About 40 B.C., Herod the Great had the temple destroyed piece by piece and rebuilt. That became known as Herod's Temple. Titus, a Roman general, laid siege to Jerusalem in A.D. 70. The Jews didn't trust his promises not to destroy it, so they burned the temple rather than allow it to fall into the hands of unbelievers.

Today the Temple Mount, the site of the old Jewish temple, houses the Muslim mosque called the Dome of the Rock. The Temple Mount sits on Mount Moriah, where it is believed Abraham expressed to God his willingness to sacrifice his son Isaac.

Since the birth of Israel as a nation in 1948, millions of dollars have been collected from around the world for the rebuilding of the temple. Many believe it will be even more spectacular than in the days of Solomon.

"It looks good," Judd said. "But what does this mean to the kids at Nicolae High?"

"That's where my stuff comes in," John said. "With a little help from Bruce, I show how this whole thing was prophesied in the Bible. Everything from the disappearances to Carpathia's covenant signing with Israel."

"Perfect," Judd said. "Now the hard part. We have to figure another way to get the *Underground* into their hands."

At Northside Detention Center Vicki was searched and relieved of her clothes, purse, Bible, and wrist messenger. "You won't need a watch in here," a matron told her. They gave her a toothbrush, a comb, and deodorant, along with a drab coverall, the uniform of the center.

"You don't have anything in navy, do you?" Vicki said.

The guard didn't smile. She led Vicki through a series of musty rooms to the residence wing. Six beds filled each room.

"Breakfast is at seven o'clock sharp," the

guard snapped. "Get up late, you don't eat. Chores every day, before and after classes. Free time in the afternoon before dinner at five. Lights out at nine. Got it?"

"I guess," Vicki said. "Can I make a phone call?"

"No calls," the guard said. "We have recreation on Saturday afternoons. That's where everybody is now. Be in the dining hall in half an hour."

Vicki sat on the bed. Paint chips littered the floor. A wasp buzzed at the grimy window. She opened the top drawer of a rickety night-stand and found a Bible. It was in bad shape. *Probably stolen from some motel,* she thought.

She found Psalm 91 and read:

"He who dwells in the secret place of the Most High shall abide under the shadow of the Almighty. I will say of the Lord, 'He is my refuge and my fortress; My God, in Him I will trust. . . .' A thousand may fall at your side, and ten thousand at your right hand; but it shall not come near you. . . . No evil shall befall you, nor shall any plague come near your dwelling; for He shall give His angels charge over you, to keep you in all your ways."

When Vicki awoke the next morning the rest of the girls were asleep. They had been up late talking after lights-out. She was excited about the "religious service" she'd seen advertised on the bulletin board near the dining hall, so she quietly dressed and found the chapel.

Fifteen girls scattered around a tiny room. They sat on folding chairs. The leader was Chaplain Cindy, a young woman with a forced smile. She looked down most of the time, perhaps because most of the girls were nodding off.

Vicki couldn't believe what she was hearing.

"God is love, and love comes from God. He is in each of you, and if you want his light, you must embrace him. I encourage you to search for God in your own way. Become yourself as much as you can, and you will grow ever closer to the Divine."

When Chaplain Cindy finished, she asked if anyone had a question or comment.

Vicki raised her hand. "I don't think God is really in all of us," she said.

A murmur spread among the girls.

"If God had been *in* us, we wouldn't still be here. The truth is, Jesus came back for his own, and we all got left behind," Vicki continued.

"Shut up."

"Yeah, stupid, sit down."

"Quiet," Chaplain Cindy said. "What's your name?"

"Vicki."

"What we try to accomplish here, Vicki, is oneness. This is not church per se. We come together in unity as part of the new movement of faith around the world."

"You mean Nicolae Carpathia's new religion."

"He's an inspired and wonderful leader," Chaplain Cindy gushed. "He follows the tenets of all the great religious teachers, including the one you mentioned."

"Jesus said that he was the *only* way to God," Vicki said. She tried to look up John 14:6, but before she could find it, she was hooted down.

Chaplain Cindy asked for order. "It's clear to me that Nicolae Carpathia is a Christian man," Chaplain Cindy said.

"You've got to be kidding," Vicki said.

"Of course! He lives by Christian principles. He's always concerned for the greater good."

Vicki was angry. She tried to steer the conversation back to Jesus, but there were more hoots as Vicki finally left the chapel.

She returned to a commotion in her room. Her roommates stood around Alice Weems, the director of NDC.

"I can smell it," Mrs. Weems said. "One of you confesses right now, or you all get punished. What's it gonna be?"

One of the girls pointed at Vicki. "It was her! She brought the weed with her when she came in yesterday."

Mrs. Weems looked at Vicki. "Well?"

"I don't know what you're talking about," Vicki said.

"Where did she stash it, Janie?" Weems said.

"In the top drawer," Janie said. "She was pretending to read some book in there."

Mrs. Weems grabbed the Bible and rifled through it until four crudely rolled cigarettes fell from a hole cut in pages in the back. She held the cigarettes up gingerly and sniffed at them.

"Come with me," she said to Vicki.

After church Sunday, Judd met Bruce in his study.

"Do we need to move?" Judd said. "If Handlesman knows where we are, I don't want to stick around the house."

"Stay put," Bruce said.

"That's it? Just stay put? After the stuff he said to you the other night?"

"Don't worry about me," Bruce said. "I can take care of myself. And you'll have to trust me. Now I have some other urgent news."

Bruce told Judd that his friend Rayford Steele had become the pilot of *Air Force One*, the plane now used by Nicolae Carpathia, the United Nations secretary-general. According to Steele, Carpathia planned to claim that plane as his own, and the pilot with it. In addition to that, *Global Weekly* writer Buck Williams had been trying to set up a meeting with the two witnesses at the Wailing Wall.

"I'd love to be there," Judd said. "The media mostly ignores them now. I wish we could get the word out about the witnesses."

"You just may have your chance," Bruce said.

"What do you mean?"

"I'll tell you later," Bruce said. "The other urgent news concerns Vicki. I found out where she was taken and tried to see her, but they don't allow visitors in the first few days."

"I've tried to send her messages," Judd said, "but I don't think they're getting through."

"Keep praying for her," Bruce said. "I've heard disturbing things about that center."

Janie stared at the floor as she and Vicki sat in Mrs. Weems's cluttered office.

"What's your last name?" Vicki asked the girl.

"What's it to ya?"

"Look, we both know I didn't hide those joints in the Bible. But either way, I'm going to be blamed for it. I just like to know who I'm up against."

Janie scowled at Vicki. "McCanyon," she said finally.

"How long you been here?"

"A year. I got sent here for gettin' drunk. Now I'm into drugs. Go figure."

Mrs. Weems's heels clacked on the tile as she entered and cocked an arm against her hip.

"Janie, you know what happens if I find out these were yours."

"Yes, ma'am."

"You," she said to Vicki, "what do you have to say for yourself?"

Something made Vicki hold her tongue.

"I'll take that as an admission," Mrs. Weems said. "Since it's your first offense, I'll go easy. Five days in solitary confinement."

Mrs. Weems told them both to sit tight while she left to take a call.

Janie glanced sheepishly at Vicki. "Look, we do what we gotta do to get by," Janie said. "Better you than me in solitary."

"You've been there?"

"A few times." Janie squirmed. "Why didn't you put up a fight?"

"Who'd believe me? Weems knows I was searched when I got here."

"You mad at me?" Janie said.

Vicki was stunned that Janie was worried about that. "Of course, but I can let it go."

"You're strange, Vicki."

Mrs. Weems's heels clacked again.

"Someday I'll tell you why," Vicki said.

"Maybe tonight," Janie said. "I've got kitchen duty this week. I'll see if I can bring your plate."

"Back to your room, McCanyon," Mrs. Weems said. "Byrne, you're this way."

Before Bruce began their Bible teaching for the evening, Chloe Steele gave an update about her father, pilot Rayford Steele. Rayford's first assignment was flying Nicolae Carpathia to the treaty signing in Israel.

"Does Carpathia know your dad's a Christian?" Ryan said.

"He does now," Chloe said. "He met

Carpathia in New York. When my dad had the chance, he told Carpathia straight-out that he was a believer in Christ."

"Wow," Ryan said. "I hope that doesn't get him in trouble."

Chloe asked everyone to pray for Buck Williams as well. All she would say was that Buck was traveling and would be in a very dangerous situation in the next few days.

As Bruce began his teaching, Judd felt his wrist messenger buzz. "Meet me tonight at nine at school" the message read. "Don't ask questions."

FOUR

Witnesses to History

BRUCE seemed excited but cautious as the meeting continued. Lionel, Ryan, John, and Mark soaked in every word as Bruce taught more about prophecy.

When the teaching time was over, Judd handed Bruce a fresh copy of the *Underground.* Bruce scanned the small print and gave a low whistle. "Can I share more about Buck?" Bruce asked Chloe. She nodded.

He said Buck Williams had met with Rabbi Tsion Ben-Judah, a brilliant Jewish scholar who had searched various holy books for the identity of the Messiah. Buck's aim was to get an interview with the two witnesses, and the rabbi got him through the tight security around the Wailing Wall.

"As they neared the crowd, Buck realized that each person present was hearing the witnesses in his or her own language!"

"Just like in Acts," Ryan said, "where all

those tongues things came down and hit them in the head."

Bruce smiled. "Buck says a man suddenly raced through the crowd with an automatic weapon, yelling that he was on a mission from Allah. When he was within five feet of the two witnesses, he fell back like he had hit an invisible wall. One of the witnesses shouted that no one was to come near the servants of the Most High God. The other breathed fire from his mouth that killed the man instantly."

"Was Buck all right?" Judd said.

"More than all right. Dr. Ben-Judah actually talked to the witnesses. He and Buck met with them alone later that night."

"Wow," Lionel said. "What did they say?"

"Listen to this," Bruce said, turning on his answering machine. "Buck recorded the entire conversation and played it to me over the phone. The first one is Moishe, and the other is Eli."

"Many years ago," Moishe said, "there was a man of the Pharisees named Nicodemus, a ruler of the Jews. Like you, this man came to Jesus by night."

Rabbi Ben-Judah whispered, "Eli and Moishe, we know that you come from God;

for no one can do these signs that you do unless God is with him."

Eli spoke. "Most assuredly, I say to you, unless one is born again, he cannot see the kingdom of God."

"How can a man be born when he is old?" Rabbi Ben-Judah said.

"This is straight out of the Bible," Ryan said. "I remember it from one of our studies. Cool."

"Shhhh," Lionel said.

Moishe answered, "Most assuredly, I say to you, unless one is born of water and the Spirit, he cannot enter the kingdom of God. That which is born of the flesh is flesh, and that which is born of the Spirit is spirit. Do not marvel that I said to you, 'You must be born again.'"

Eli spoke up again: "The wind blows where it wishes, and you hear the sound of it, but cannot tell where it comes from and where it goes. So is everyone who is born of the Spirit."

Right on cue, the rabbi said, "How can these things be?"

"Are you the teacher of Israel, and do not know these things?" Moishe said. "Most assuredly, I say to you, we speak what we know and testify what we have seen, and you do not receive our witness. If we have told you earthly things and you do not believe, how will you believe if we tell you heavenly things?"

The voices sounded like prophets right out of the Old Testament. "No one has ascended to heaven but He who came down from heaven," Eli said, "that is, the Son of Man who is in heaven. And as Moses lifted up the serpent in the wilderness, even so must the Son of Man be lifted up, that whoever believes in Him should not perish but have eternal life. For God so loved the world that He gave His only begotten Son, that whoever believes in Him should not perish but have everlasting life."

The kids sat shaking their heads as Moishe concluded his message.

"For God did not send his Son into the world to condemn the world, but that the world through him might be saved. He who believes in Him is not condemned; but he who does not believe is condemned already, because he has not believed in the name of the only begotten Son of God."

Rabbi Ben-Judah sounded animated now. "And what is the condemnation?"

In unison the witnesses said, "That the light has already come into the world."

"And how did men miss it?"

"Men loved darkness rather than light."

"Why?"

"Because their deeds were evil."

"God forgive us," the rabbi said.

And the two witnesses said, "God forgive you. Thus ends our message."

"Incredible," Ryan said.

"I thought most rabbis were skeptical of these preachers," John said.

Bruce turned off the machine. "Yes. But people are turning. Buck said Rabbi Ben-Judah took him to the Dome of the Rock and translated the Hebrew graffiti there. It said, 'Come, Messiah' and 'Deliver us,' and 'Come in triumph.' The Jewish people have been longing for Messiah for thousands of years. Buck says the Muslims have even built a cemetery near the Dome."

"So?" Mark said.

"Jewish tradition says that in the end times, Messiah and Elijah will lead the Jews to the temple in triumph through the gate from the east. But Elijah is a priest, and walking through a graveyard would defile him, so they put a cemetery there to make the triumphal entry impossible."

"Does this Ben-Judah guy believe Jesus is the Messiah?" John said.

"We'll find out tomorrow. He gives his conclusions on a live international TV broadcast."

The solitary confinement room was windowless, and the air stale and muggy. A large black spider hung in one corner near the high ceiling, spinning a web. Vicki tried to kill it by throwing a shoe, but gave up. If she knocked it down she'd have to find it and step on it, so she left it alone.

Late in the afternoon she heard a knock on the door. A slit opened enough to fit a dinner plate through.

"Sorry, this is all they'd let me give you," Janie said. "I put some extra peas on there."

Vicki didn't want to be ungrateful, but she wouldn't have given the meal even to Phoenix. And she hated peas.

"Weems will lock me up next to you if I'm not back soon," Janie said. "What were you going to say in the office? Why didn't you rat on me?"

Vicki held the flap open so she could see Janie's bloodshot eyes. Drugs made her look years older.

"This was something God wanted me to do," Vicki said.

"God?" Janie said. "Oh boy."

"Maybe I'm in here just to show you how much God loves you."

"OK, gotta go," Janie said.

"No, wait. Just a second."

Vicki quickly told how she had become a Christian after losing her family in the disappearances. "What I did for you today was sort of like what Jesus did for me," Vicki said.

"Yeah, whatever." Janie turned to leave.

Vicki called after her. "I didn't do anything wrong, right?"

Janie stopped. "Right."

"You were the guilty one, right?"

"Uh, OK, maybe."

"I'm taking your punishment, paying for what you did. That's what Jesus did for me. For you, too . . ."

"How do you know all this stuff?"

"It's all in the Bible. Get me one, and I'll show you."

"Did you have one with you when you came in?" Janie said.

"Yeah, a little one," Vicki said. "But don't—"

"Shh," Janie said, pushing the flap closed quietly.

"I wish I could be there to hear the witnesses myself," Judd said.

"It would be great if we could get their message to more people," John said.

"We could put the audio on the Internet," Mark said. "Or maybe Mr. Williams could get us some video."

"It's interesting you bring this up," Bruce said. "I'm looking for a volunteer."

"For what?" Ryan said. "I'll do it."

"Slow down," Bruce said. "I feel strongly that God wants me to take the small group model we've begun here and replicate it overseas."

"What's *replicate* mean?" Ryan said.

"Do the same thing over there as here," Lionel said.

"I want to go to Israel, to the Wailing Wall, to see the witnesses," Bruce continued. "I want to see where these prophecies came from. God's work in human history began there. Whatever he has for our future will begin there as well. I'd like one of you to go with me."

Vicki wished for anything to pass the time. She didn't even have pen or paper. She slept as much as she could and kept an eye on the spider when she was awake.

Her dozing made her less sleepy, and just before lights-out she worried she wouldn't sleep. Then she heard something in the hall-way. Was Mrs. Weems paying her a visit? It was only a matter of time.

The loudspeaker crackled "lights-out," and the room went dark. Her plate from lunch slid from outside the door, and then the flap creaked open. Something dropped on the floor.

Maybe it was a trick. Or maybe a smoke bomb or more evidence planted to get her in deeper trouble. Vicki sat on the edge of the bed, her feet tucked underneath her, and tried to adjust to the darkness. A bit of light from under the door was partially blocked.

Vicki felt around on the floor until she found a grocery bag. Inside she felt her New Testament and something else. Her wrist messenger! Tears welled up.

When she could see clearly, she noticed a

new message. It was hours old. "OK, Vicki, we'll meet you at nine at the school."

"Sure will be great to see Vicki," Mark said.

Judd had a queasy feeling about the meeting, like something wasn't right.

"Why didn't you say anything to Bruce?" Mark said. "He'd probably want to see Vicki too."

"If she wanted Bruce there, she would have said something," Judd said as he neared the school parking lot.

"Pull over!" John shouted.

"What's wrong?" Judd said.

"Another message from Vicki. She's still at NDC!"

Judd screeched to a halt and saw headlights switch on in the distance.

"The other message had to have been a trap," Lionel said. "They're trying to catch us."

"But it doesn't make sense," Mark said. "Handlesman knows Vicki was at your place. He could just come over and get us."

"Uh-oh," Mark said. "Maybe they're at the house gathering the evidence. Ryan's at home with Phoenix. They might be questioning him right now."

Judd backed up and gunned the engine. The headlights in his rearview mirror faded as Judd did a one-eighty.

An unmarked police cruiser with lights flashing blocked Judd's driveway. Ryan was on the front step talking with someone, while others from the neighborhood milled about. Judd drove past and parked a few doors down.

"We're fried," John said.

"What's going on?" Judd asked a neighbor.

"Somebody said something about a burglary," he said.

"Stay here," Judd told the others. He hurried to the front steps.

"Hey, Judd." Ryan grinned.

The officer turned, and Judd was relieved to see Sergeant Tom Fogarty. Judd and the others had helped the Chicago police officer crack a drug-and-burglary ring shortly after the disappearances. Ryan had called him in desperation.

"Looks like you had a little excitement while you were out," Sergeant Fogarty said. "Ryan says he was by himself, and somebody tried to get in. Big guy."

"Do you know who it was?" Judd said.

"Didn't get a look at his face," Ryan said. "But I'll know who he is when I see him."

"How's that?" Judd said.

"The perp got in the front door, and Ryan whacked him with a golf club."

"Yeah, and while he was kinda groggy, Phoenix bit him on the arm," Ryan added.

"You might want to get that door fixed pretty soon," Sergeant Fogarty said.

"I will," Judd said. "First thing after school."

FIVE

Treaty with the Devil

MONDAY morning the *Underground* made it into Nicolae High the back way. Judd went through the front and was searched, like all the other kids, while John and Mark took their stashes of paper to the side of the school. Judd pulled the small bundles through a window.

The format of this edition of the *Underground* was different. The kids had limited themselves to two pages and had shrunk the type. They cut the bright blue paper to hand-bill size and took it to the cafeteria.

Judd, John, and Mark left stacks of what looked like an advertisement from a popular burger place. When students picked them up, however, they found the truth about the treaty with Israel.

"If somebody doesn't bite soon," Mark said, "I'm gonna bust."

"Don't worry," John said, "it'll spread."

A girl in a running suit grabbed a flyer and walked back to a table, where she read it to her friends. Soon another girl came to pick up a flyer, then another. Judd moved to a side entrance of the cafeteria and watched in delight.

"Judd, I've been looking for you," Vicki's friend Shelly said. Judd was wary. She had betrayed Vicki.

"How's it goin', Shelly," Judd said.

"The question is, how's Vicki?" she said.

"How would I know?"

"I thought you were kinda hangin' together."

Wary of yet another trap, Judd shrugged. "A little," he said.

"I feel awful. Please tell her I want to make it up to her, OK?"

"If I see her," Judd said.

"Oh, and nice job on the *Underground*. I mean, I know it was you guys."

"Uh . . ." Judd avoided her eyes.

"Watch this," she said. She grabbed a stack of flyers and handed them out.

"Can we trust her?" Mark said.

"I'm not sure," Judd said. "Why don't you keep an eye on her?"

Mrs. Jenness's voice came over the loud-speaker. "All students report to the auditorium. The video of the historic treaty ceremony earlier this morning in Israel will be played in its entirety."

The auditorium was filling as Judd and John arrived. Several students carried copies of the *Underground*. The audience focused on a huge screen broadcasting CNN's coverage.

"The signing ceremony was abruptly moved to the Knesset earlier this morning, Israel time," the CNN reporter said. "Some say Nicolae Carpathia was not happy with what the two preachers were saying at the Wailing Wall. What you hear behind me may be the reason. . . ."

The camera zoomed in on Eli and Moishe. With long-range, directional microphones, CNN picked up their decrying the injustice of the signing.

"This covenant signals an unholy alliance!" Moishe shouted.

"O Israel," Eli said, "you who missed your Messiah the first time have embraced a leader who denies the existence of God!"

Some kids laughed at the two, but others looked at the *Underground* and pointed to the screen. CNN flashed to the Knesset.

Judd felt helpless. No one could stem the tide of history. Bruce Barnes had taught him that there would be 144,000 Jewish converts and that the first would come from the Holy

Land. The Bible said the converts would come from every part of the globe and would reap an incredible harvest—perhaps a billion souls.

Judd perked up when Buck Williams was announced as a dignitary in attendance. The loudest applause was reserved for the last five men: the chief rabbi of Israel, the Nobel Prize–winning botanist Chaim Rosenzweig of Israel, the prime minister of Israel, the president of the United States, and the secretary-general of the Global Community. As the applause crescendoed for Nicolae Carpathia, Mrs. Jenness took the podium.

"This is a great day for world peace," she said. "I hope you understand the historic moment you're witnessing. Please hold your applause so everyone can hear."

John caught Judd's eye and shook his head. "I'll try to contain myself."

"I just hope some of these people read the truth in the *Underground*," Judd said.

On the screen Nicolae Carpathia recognized those who had helped reach the agreement and ended by introducing "the Honorable Gerald Fitzhugh, president of the United States of America, the greatest friend Israel has ever had."

President Fitzhugh rose to thunderous

applause; then Nicolae Carpathia beckoned him to the microphone.

"The last thing I want to do at a moment like this," President Fitzhugh said, "is to detract in any way from the occasion at hand. However, with your kind indulgence, I would like to make a couple of brief points.

"First, it has been a privilege to see what Nicolae Carpathia has done in just a few short weeks. I am certain we all agree that the world is a more loving, peaceful place because of him."

President Fitzhugh pledged his support to global disarmament. "I support the secretary-general's plan without reservation. It's a stroke of genius. We will lead the way to the rapid destruction of 90 percent of our weapons and the donation of the other 10 percent to Global Community, under Mr. Carpathia's direction.

"As a tangible expression of my personal support and that of our nation as a whole, we have also gifted Global Community with the brand-new *Air Force One*."

"There goes Rayford Steele," John said. "He'll be flying the Antichrist anywhere he wants to go."

President Fitzhugh dramatically paused. "Now I surrender the microphone to the man of destiny, the leader whose current title does not do justice to the extent of his influence, to my personal friend and compatriot, Nicolae Carpathia!"

Wild applause broke out in Jerusalem and at Nicolae High. Bruce had told Judd he thought President Fitzhugh wasn't pleased with the way Carpathia had taken over, but his speech certainly cleared that up.

Other leaders spoke of Nicolae Carpathia in glowing terms. He was a gift from God, they said. Several decorative pens were produced as television, film, video, and still cameras zeroed in on the signers. The pens were passed back and forth. There were handshakes, embraces, and kisses on both cheeks.

Judd marveled at what the kids had written. A covenant had been struck. God's chosen people had signed a deal with the devil. The seven-year "week" predicted in the Bible had begun. The Tribulation.

Mark slipped into Judd and John's row; he was out of breath. "Good news and bad news," he said. "Shelly just had a conversation with Handlesman. I think we're in trouble."

"What's the good news?" John said.

"You should see the bruise on Handlesman's head!"

Vicki awoke to the door flap creaking. Janie was back.

"I saw you didn't eat anything last night," she whispered, "so I found a couple of fresh biscuits."

Vicki took them and bit into them eagerly. "Thanks," she said. "These are great."

Janie said Vicki's Bible and watch hadn't been in the property room but in Mrs. Weems's office. "Nobody else was using them, so why shouldn't you?"

"You're taking a big risk, Janie. Be careful."

Janie looked into Vicki's eyes. "I was thinking about what you said last night."

Janie gasped, and the flap closed. "I'm sorry, I'm sorry," Janie said. "I was just giving her breakfast!"

Keys jangled, and Vicki's door swung open. Mrs. Weems bounded in, dragging Janie. "Solitary means you're alone," Mrs. Weems said. "You don't talk to anybody, you don't—"

Mrs. Weems swept the Bible and wrist messenger off the bed. She stomped on the messenger, smashing it to bits. "So much for your watch," she said.

She threw Janie toward the bed. "Now it's

your turn for solitary, McCanyon! Byrne, you come with me."

Vicki picked up the Bible and followed the woman through a waiting room. A nicely dressed couple looked up and then quickly looked away.

"Get your stuff together," Mrs. Weems said after she closed the door.

"I only have this," Vicki said, holding her Bible.

"That was stolen from my office!" Mrs. Weems took the Bible and threw it in the trash. "You must know somebody important. You're getting transferred out of here to the Stein family. I don't know why they agreed to take you, but they did. Listen, one wrong move and you're back here. And believe me, Byrne, you don't wanna come back."

By the end of the treaty-signing coverage on TV, teachers were confiscating the *Underground.* Judd saw some students stuff them in their pockets.

One student raised a hand. "Weren't we supposed to see some rabbi's report too?"

"That's been canceled due to inappropriate content," Mrs. Jenness said.

"Wonder what was so inappropriate?" John said.

In class, students regarded Carpathia as everything from "cool" to "the greatest leader the world has ever known."

"I like what he's done with the media," a reporter from the school newspaper said. "I think we're going to see a lot less bias and more honest reporting now," she added.

"Interesting," the teacher said. "Many see it differently. Carpathia has accomplished something no one ever thought would happen. He's purchased newspapers, radio stations, television networks, satellite communications outlets—you name it. The Cable News Network, the Columbia Broadcast System, Time-Warner, Disney, *Newsweek*,—they all now come under the auspices of the Global Community."

Judd's heart sank. The most evil man on the earth was gaining more control. No one could stop him.

SIX

The Rabbi's Message

MITCHELL and Judith Stein were a Jewish couple who had become foster parents after the loss of their daughter.

"How did she die?" Vicki said.

Silence.

"I'm sorry," she said. "I—"

"It's all right," Mr. Stein said. "It's just difficult for us to talk about."

"What was her name?" Vicki said.

The Steins didn't answer at first. Then Mrs. Stein whispered, "Chaya."

Mrs. Stein showed Vicki to a bright, cheery bedroom with a huge canopy bed and three windows that looked out on a manicured lawn. Exhausted, Vicki took a nap and was awakened by noise downstairs. She crept to the banister and watched a man on television speak about the Jewish Messiah.

Though Vicki had never seen him, she

knew this must be the rabbi Bruce had
mentioned. For three years he had worked
on a government project. The assignment
was to read sacred books, including the
Bible, and discover the identity of the Jewish
Messiah. His findings had been kept secret
until this broadcast.

"He is like every Orthodox Jew we know,"
Mr. Stein said. "He will tell us to be patient.
Messiah is yet to come. We have heard this
many times."

He aimed the remote control.

"Wait," Vicki said as she bounded down
the staircase. "Can I watch that?"

"You are interested?" he said.

"Very."

He shrugged and left it on.

"Thank you, Vicki," Mrs. Stein said. "I
would like to see this myself."

The words *Dr. Tsion Ben-Judah* flashed at
the bottom of the screen. He was sitting on
the edge of the table where he had displayed
the several-hundred-page conclusion to his
research study. He said he would tackle the
question of Messiah in the broadcast. Is Messiah a real person? Has he come, or is he yet
to come? The camera zoomed in on Dr.
Ben-Judah's impressive features.

"I promise to not bore you with statistics,
but we believe there are at least 109 separate

and distinct prophecies Messiah must fulfill. They require a man so unusual and a life so unique that they eliminate all pretenders."

"He may proclaim Nicolae Carpathia as Messiah," Mrs. Stein said. "Who else could have done what he has in such a short time?"

Vicki shuddered.

"The very first qualification of Messiah, accepted by our scholars from the beginning, is that he should be born of the seed of a woman, not the seed of a man like all other human beings. We know now that women do not possess 'seed.' The man provides the seed for the woman's egg. And so this must be a supernatural birth, as foretold in Isaiah 7:14, 'Therefore the Lord Himself will give you a sign: Behold, the virgin shall conceive and bear a Son, and shall call His name Immanuel.'"

Rabbi Ben-Judah further qualified Messiah as a descendant of David, born in Bethlehem, and rejected by his own people.

Mr. Stein reddened. "I know where this is going," he said, "and I do not like it."

"Listen to him," Mrs. Stein said. "He is quoting from our scriptures, isn't he?"

After clearly explaining what the Bible said for nearly an hour, the rabbi said, "Let me close by saying that the three years I have

invested in searching the sacred writings of
Moses and the prophets have been the most
rewarding of my life. I expanded my study to
books of history and other sacred writings,
including the New Testament of the Gentiles,
combing every record I could find to see if
anyone has ever lived up to the messianic
qualifications. . . ."

"Do you see?" Mr. Stein said. "He is basing
his findings on erroneous material!"

"How can you decide he is wrong if you
won't even listen to him?" Mrs. Stein said.

"Was there one born in Bethlehem of a
virgin," Ben-Judah continued, "a descendant
of King David, traced back to our father
Abraham, who was taken to Egypt, called
back to minister in Galilee, preceded by a
forerunner, rejected by God's own people,
betrayed for thirty pieces of silver, pierced
without breaking a bone, buried with the
rich, and resurrected?

"According to one of the greatest of all
Hebrew prophets, Daniel, there would be
exactly 483 years between the decree to
rebuild the wall and the city of Jerusalem 'in
troublesome times' before the Messiah
would be cut off for the sins of the people."

Ben-Judah looked directly into the camera.
"Exactly 483 years after the rebuilding of

Jerusalem and its walls, Jesus Christ of Nazareth offered himself to the nation of Israel."

"Blasphemy!" Mr. Stein shouted. "I'm turning it off!"

"What are you afraid of?" Mrs. Stein said.

"I will not subject myself to such trash!"

"Your daughter believed in this 'trash.'"

The rabbi continued. "Jesus rode into the city on a donkey to the rejoicing of the people, just as the prophet Zechariah had predicted: 'Rejoice greatly, O daughter of Zion! Shout, O daughter of Jerusalem! Behold, your King is coming to you; He is just and having salvation, lowly and riding on a donkey, a colt, the foal of a donkey.'"

"Maybe Chaya was right," Mrs. Stein said. "Maybe we should have listened while we had the chance."

"You will never use her name in this house again," Mr. Stein said. "Never!"

Vicki stood as the rabbi concluded, thrilled at the message he proclaimed. "Jesus Christ is the Messiah! There can be no other option. I had come to this answer but was afraid to act on it, and I was almost too late. Jesus came to rapture his church, to take them with him to heaven as he said he would. I was not among them because I wavered. But I have since received him as my Savior. He is coming back in seven years! Be ready!"

Dr. Ben-Judah gave a number to call for more information, but there seemed to be commotion in the TV studio.

"*Yeshua ben Yosef*, Jesus son of Joseph, is *Yeshua Hamashiach!*" the rabbi shouted quickly. "Jesus is the Messiah!"

The screen went blank.

Bruce described the message by Rabbi Tsion Ben-Judah as nothing short of miraculous. It had been broadcast live around the world. Because his findings had been kept secret, the Global Community hadn't restricted the broadcast, but Nicolae Carpathia had to be seething.

Later the four kids learned that Buck Williams was able to help the rabbi escape the television studio. Many in his own country wanted to kill the rabbi for his beliefs.

"The most exciting news is that Eli and Moishe have invited Dr. Ben-Judah to address a meeting of new believers in a large stadium in Israel. They have pledged their protection for the rabbi as he proclaims the Good News."

Mrs. Stein knocked on Vicki's door that night.

"We don't normally have outbursts like this," she said, entering the room. "But ever since we lost our daughter, things have not been the same."

Vicki nodded. "Chaya is in heaven, you know."

"I can't talk now," Mrs. Stein said. "Please, just know that you cannot bring it up with Mitchell."

"Can you tell me if I'll be able to go back to my old school?" Vicki said. "Or call my friends?"

"We were given strict guidelines. No contact with your friends. You'll attend Global Community High in Barrington."

"Why can't I talk with them?" Vicki said. "That doesn't seem fair."

Mrs. Stein looked away. "Life isn't fair."

As she turned to leave, Vicki said, "Can I ask what you thought about what the rabbi said?"

Mrs. Stein stopped and nodded. "I have been thinking about his words all evening. He seemed such an honest man. So learned. It is hard for me to believe he is trying to deceive us."

"I don't think he is," Vicki said.

"Sometimes I wonder if—"

"Judith?" Mr. Stein was at the door.

His wife quickly excused herself. But as she backed away, she held Vicki's gaze and opened the end-table drawer.

As soon as the door was shut, Vicki looked in the drawer and found a spiral notebook. "Chaya's Journal" was scrawled on the front cover. Vicki felt guilty opening it, but clearly Mrs. Stein had pointed her to it.

"The last thing I want to do is hurt Mom and Dad," Vicki read, "but I can't hide from the truth of what Tom is saying. I know there's something to this, but I don't want to believe it."

Vicki picked her way through the pages to find out who Tom was. She found an entry describing him as a "Jesus jerk." Tom had talked with Chaya about Christ.

"I told him, 'Look, I'm a Jew, lay off!' I think it worked. I haven't seen him for two days."

But it hadn't worked. Tom kept talking with her, discussing Jesus and the Bible.

"I want to dismiss this as a fable, a fairy tale by people who want to make Jesus who they want him to be. But I don't want to make a mistake, either. What if his claims are real? Didn't he fulfill all those predictions? If I can disprove his miracles, I can get Tom off my back and get on with my life."

From the journal it was clear. The more

Chaya investigated, the more convinced she became that Jesus was exactly who he said he was.

Then Vicki read something that sent a chill through her. "If my mom or dad ever find out about this, I'm dead."

Before the boys left Bruce's office, Mark brought up the militia movement. "They've been able to stockpile weapons," he said. "If there's any chance for freedom from Carpathia, it rests with them."

Bruce frowned.

Mark continued. "A guy I know says the president is cooperating with them. What if it's true? If they have President Fitzhugh's support, they can't be all wrong."

"There may be a place for military strength," Bruce said. "But I would hate to see you get involved with them."

"But why? If somebody doesn't stand up to Carpathia, we'll all be serving the devil! I don't see why you're against this."

"Our battle is different," Bruce said, flipping open his Bible. "Ephesians 6 says, 'Be strong in the Lord and in the power of His might. Put on the whole armor of God, that you may be able to stand against the wiles of the devil. For we do not wrestle against flesh and blood, but against principalities, against powers, against the rulers of the darkness of this age, against spiritual hosts of wickedness in the heavenly places.'"

"Why can't I be a Christian *and* fight with weapons?" Mark said. "The Bible is full of examples."

"Just be sure," Bruce said, "that you're doing this God's way. Zechariah 4:6 says, 'Not by might nor by power, but by My Spirit, says the Lord of hosts.'"

The last entry in Chaya's journal showed that she had studied about Jesus and concluded that he was a person of history. Chaya believed that the miracles in the New Testament were real.

"If I believe that Jesus is the Messiah," she wrote, *"I turn my back on my parents, my heritage, my ancestors, my friends. But if Jesus is the Messiah, I'm not turning my back on the God of Abraham, Isaac, and Jacob. I will meet with Tom tonight. I need to settle it once and for all."*

Vicki looked at the date on that final entry. It was the same night as the disappearances!

SEVEN

Chaya's Story

THE E-mail reaction alone to the *Underground* kept the Young Trib Force busy until late Monday night. A few of the E-mails called the *Underground* a joke. More than fifty said they wanted a Bible. Judd and John answered each E-mail with a gospel outline and information about New Hope Village Church.

Ryan scurried to his hidden cache of Bibles. Judd still didn't know how many Ryan had recovered, but from Ryan's description, it had to be hundreds. Ryan made three trips and had all fifty Bibles in the back of Judd's car by midnight.

Judd knew he had to be careful. An infiltrator could pose as an eager student. So Judd made the drop points off campus. He delayed sending the E-mails as he went around town delivering copies of the Bible.

He heard a scream outside and found Lionel and Ryan wrestling on the driveway.

"He's crazy, man!" Lionel said as Judd separated them.

"You're the one who's crazy!" Ryan screamed.

Judd took them into the house. Lionel said he was stuffing the response packets into the Bibles when Ryan told him to leave them alone.

"He got all territorial on me," Lionel said. "I just put the envelopes in. He jumped me."

"He just took over," Ryan said. "He acted like those Bibles were his."

Judd asked Lionel to finish outside while he took Ryan to his room. He wanted to lay into Ryan good, but he held back. Something else was wrong.

"I know Lionel can get on your nerves," Judd said. "But he didn't deserve to be attacked. What's going on?"

Ryan pulled Phoenix close to him. "I don't know. He was being a jerk." Finally the dam broke, and the tears came. "Why did Vicki have to go away?" he sobbed.

"She's a good friend," Judd said. "I miss her too."

"And now you and Bruce are leaving, and who knows when you'll come back. Or *if* you'll come back!"

"That's not a done deal," Judd said.

"Bruce wants you to go, and you know it!"

Judd took Ryan by the shoulders. "Listen to me. When you came here I promised God I'd take care of you. I hadn't paid attention to my brother and sister, so when you came along I felt like God was giving me a second chance. If Bruce wants me to go and you don't, I'll let somebody else go."

Ryan looked stunned. "I don't want you to stay because of me. I don't want to be a wuss."

"You're not," Judd said. "I can't imagine how hard this has been for you."

"Thanks," Ryan said. "I want you to go. I'll be OK."

"You sure?" Judd said.

Ryan nodded. "I gotta go apologize to Lionel."

The next day, while in the car with Mrs. Stein, Vicki asked again, "Can you tell me how she died?"

The woman hesitated. "It is a deep wound" was all she would say.

At Mrs. Stein's doctor's appointment, she asked Vicki if she could trust her to stay in the waiting room.

"Of course," Vicki said.

As soon as Mrs. Stein left to see the doctor, Vicki approached the receptionist.

"Have the Steins been coming here a long time?" she said.

"For years."

"Chaya too?"

The receptionist stiffened. "Why?"

"I'm just curious. How old was she?"

"About eighteen. She just started university last year. Bright girl. You have to be to get into the University of Chicago."

"How did she die?" Vicki said.

The receptionist stopped typing, looked to see if anyone was listening, and beckoned Vicki closer.

Just then Mrs. Stein emerged, and the receptionist went back to her work.

Later, Vicki called the University of Chicago and discovered that Chaya had withdrawn from the school about the time of the disappearances. She hung up as Mr. Stein appeared.

"Who were you calling?"

"Just trying to reach a friend," she said.

"You know the rules," he said, pulling the phone cord from the jack.

Vicki combed through Chaya's old address books and calendars for clues. She finally came upon Tom's phone number and waited for her chance.

Vicki believed that Chaya came to Christ and had been raptured. But what if she had met with Tom and hadn't made a decision? Maybe she killed herself. That would explain the "deep wound" her mother spoke of. Chaya might also have died from an accident or even been murdered. Worst of all, Chaya could have been harmed by her parents.

Vicki had to know.

The next day, Vicki found her chance while shopping with Mrs. Stein. While the woman was in the dressing room, Vicki broke away and found a pay phone.

A groggy male voice answered.

"Hi, uh, who's this?" Vicki said.

"Look, if you're callin' for Tom, he's not here! He's gone, OK?"

"I figured," Vicki said. "I'm trying to find a friend of his. Do you remember his talking about Chaya?"

"The Jewish girl? Yeah."

"Do you know what happened to her?"

"No idea. She had an apartment in the Loop. Rode the train to school. That's all I know."

Vicki hurried back. At lunch she asked Mrs. Stein, "Why are you doing this for me? You didn't have to take me in. There are a hundred other girls you could help."

"We chose NDC because many who are there have given up hope," Mrs. Stein said. "I like to think I'm giving someone a chance for a better life."

"I'm not a charity case," Vicki said.

"That's not what drew us to you. Mrs. Weems said you were troubled but that you had spunk."

Vicki shook her head. She excused herself to go to the ladies' room and called directory information. There were two Chaya Steins in Chicago, but only one lived downtown. She put more coins in and dialed. A young lady answered.

"Sorry to bother you. I'm looking for some information about your roommate."

"Moved out about a month ago," the girl said.

"And her name was Chaya?"

"No, Gwen. I'm Chaya."

"You're Chaya Stein?" Vicki said.

"I am."

"The one from Barrington?"

"The same."

"But you're supposed to be dead!"

"You've been talking to my parents."

"Yes, they said you had died."

"I see," Chaya said. "And how do you know them?"

"I'm staying with them. Could we meet somewhere?"

They settled on a park not far from the Stein house.

"I'll meet you near the tennis courts Friday at noon," Chaya said.

Friday morning Vicki found Chaya's tennis racquet and asked Mrs. Stein if there were courts nearby.

"A few blocks away," Mrs. Stein said, "but I'm not supposed to let you go unsupervised."

"You don't trust me yet?"

Mrs. Stein hesitated. "All right. Go ahead. But don't be too long."

Vicki recognized Chaya immediately. "You look like your mother!"

Chaya's eyes misted. "This is hard."

Vicki apologized for reading her journal. Chaya said it was OK. Chaya asked about her parents and what they had said about her, but Vicki interrupted. "What happened with Tom that night?"

Chaya sat on a bench and took a deep breath. "We met in a coffee shop," she began. "He had a class the next morning, but he said he'd stay as long as I had questions. At that point I knew the truth. I had read all I needed, but I just hadn't made a decision. I knew my parents would take it hard if I went apostate, but—"

"What's that?" Vicki said.

"Becoming a heretic. Believing lies. Turning your back on everything you've been taught. I could have robbed a bank, gotten pregnant—whatever—and it wouldn't have been as terrible as becoming a Christian. A couple of years ago a friend of the family became a Christian, and I thought my parents would sit shivah for him on the day he was baptized."

"What's that?"

"Prayers for the dead," Chaya said. "My guess is that my parents don't even mention my name anymore, right?"

Vicki described the painful references to Chaya's name.

"Tell me about that night with Tom," Vicki said. "If you were that close to becoming a Christian, what happened?"

"He was walking me to my train. I was telling him what my parents might do if I converted. He quoted some verse and said no earthly pain was worth the loss of my soul. I wasn't so sure and turned to say so. His book bag fell to the sidewalk. His clothes lay in a heap on the ground. I screamed."

"How awful," Vicki said.

"It was like a movie," Chaya said. "People came running. They picked up his clothes and book bag, somebody tried to lift a manhole cover, but there was nothing they could do. He was gone."

"Did you know what had happened?"

"You mean the Rapture? No. Tom had told me Jesus was coming back, but we hadn't gotten that far. That night when I finally got home I watched the news about all the vanishings. I wanted to look up the verse he had talked about, but all I could remember was that it was in Matthew. I read the first sixteen chapters until I came to it: 'For what profit is it to a man if he gains the whole world, and loses his own soul?'"

"Tom had given me other materials," Chaya continued. "I read from Romans 10, 'If you confess with your mouth the Lord Jesus and believe in your heart that God has raised Him from the dead, you will be saved.' And later it says, 'For whoever calls on the name of the Lord shall be saved.' I begged God to save me. And he did."

Then Vicki told her own story, right up to

going to the NDC and being assigned to the Steins.

Chaya wept as she said that the most difficult thing in her life had been telling her parents. "My father yelled, my mother wailed, and before they closed the door behind me, they disowned me."

Vicki put a hand on her shoulder and looked past her to the street. Chaya's mother stood by her car, watching.

EIGHT

The Mole

JUDD left school early. He went home and packed and led Phoenix to the car. There was still much to do before getting to the airport. It was 2:15 P.M. Everything was going as planned.

When Chaya stood, Mrs. Stein jumped into her car and pulled away. Chaya bit her lip, then composed herself. "Come on," she said. "I'll run you home."

"I'd rather see my friends," Vicki said. "Your parents are sure to send me back to the detention center."

At 2:15 Vicki and Chaya arrived at Nicolae High and waited for the end of the school day in hopes of seeing the guys. Vicki saw a familiar face in a girls' gym class—Shelly. Vicki waved.

"I'm so glad to see you," Shelly said,

running over to the car. "Did you get my message?"

"I've been kinda out of touch for a few days," Vicki said. She introduced Chaya to Shelly.

"Are you with the foster family?" Shelly said.

"How did you know that?" Vicki said.

"From a friend. I'm really sorry about what happened. I wouldn't have done that to you for anything. But you know Mom."

Vicki nodded.

"You should have seen what the guys did with the *Underground* Monday," Shelly said.

Vicki had never told her who was involved with the paper. Could she trust Shelly? Shelly had been the one responsible for her being sent to the detention center. How did she know all these things?

"Wait right here," Shelly said. "You're not going to believe this. I'll be right back, OK?"

A few moments later Shelly burst out the door, pulling someone behind her. Vicki looked in horror. Coach Handlesman.

Judd picked up Ryan and Lionel from their school.

"You got all our stuff?" Lionel said.

"It's in the back," Judd said. "And John has a key in case you guys need anything while I'm gone."

"Your house is gonna be a ghost town," Ryan said.

Judd dropped them off at John and Mark's house by 2:45. Lionel and Ryan would stay with the boys and their aunt until Judd returned.

"What are you doing here?" Coach Handlesman said.

Vicki couldn't speak. Shelly had betrayed her again.

Mrs. Jenness and a Global Community guard were at the car. The door opened. Vicki felt numb, like in a dream. The guard pulled her from the car and whisked her inside the school.

"What's going on?" Chaya shouted. "Where are you taking her?"

Shelly ran after them but was turned back when they reached Mrs. Jenness's office. "All right, where is he?" Mrs. Jenness demanded. "Where is Judd Thompson?"

"He's not here?"

"Enough! We know you helped Thompson with that newspaper. We have proof!"

Coach Handlesman burst in. "What proof?" he shouted.

"So, you're all concerned about your little project," Mrs. Jenness said.

Vicki was confused.

"Where's Thompson?" Mrs. Jenness said, eyeing the coach.

"I don't know either," he said.

"We have the proof we need," Mrs. Jenness said as the girls' gym teacher, Mrs. Laverne Waltonen, entered. Mrs. Jenness motioned to her secretary. "Get the superintendent on the phone."

Coach Handlesman moved toward the door, but a guard blocked his way.

"We'll get to the bottom of this," Mrs. Jenness said. "And your career is in jeopardy," she added to Coach Handlesman.

"What?" Vicki said. "The coach? Why?"

"You ought to know!" Mrs. Jenness said.

"Enough!" Coach Handlesman shouted. "Leave her alone. I'll tell you everything."

Bruce, Judd, and John hit traffic as they neared O'Hare Airport. An overturned trailer had spilled its contents on the expressway. Bruce had wanted to get there an hour and a half before takeoff, but they weren't going to be close. It was nearly 4:00 P.M., and they were still miles away.

The superintendent of Global Community Schools, Gerald Pembroke, arrived at 4:05 P.M. He was a large man with thin lips, and he talked precisely. Vicki was still reeling.

Superintendent Pembroke asked where "the Thompson boy" was. Coach Handlesman looked at his watch and again said that he didn't know. Mrs. Weems arrived to escort Vicki out, but Coach Handlesman stopped her. "Vicki stays," he said. "If you want the whole story, I want her right here."

Mrs. Weems looked to Mrs. Jenness. She nodded. "Sit down. You can stay."

Coach Handlesman took the floor.

"Don't blame Vicki. And quit following her around and punishing her for something that's my fault. This is my doing, and I'm ready to take whatever punishment you want to give."

"You let an innocent girl be sent to a place like Northside?" Mr. Pembroke said.

"I'm not proud of it," Coach Handlesman said. "I'm saying I want to clear things up."

"You printed and distributed those papers yourself?" Superintendent Pembroke said.

"I'm telling you, it was my fault. I'm sure Mrs. Waltonen has told you my views."

"She said you came on pretty strong."

"It's true. I'm a born-again Christian. I want to reach as many kids as possible. That's all I have to say."

Mrs. Jenness's secretary buzzed. "Rumor has it that the Thompson kid is going to the airport. Somebody said he's headed to Israel."

Israel, Vicki thought. *Why? And who's he with?*

The Global Community guard picked up the phone. "Get me El Al Airlines at O'Hare."

Bruce and Judd consolidated their clothing as John drove. They would be allowed only two carry-on bags.

"We'll never make it on time to check our luggage," Bruce said. "We take what we can run with."

"That means we leave the recording equipment," Judd said.

"We'll have to," Bruce said.

John screeched to a halt, and the two flew into the international terminal. They were breathless when they reached the ticket counter.

Mrs. Jenness had the guard finish his phone call in the next office. The rest of the group eagerly followed. Vicki and Coach Handlesman were alone.

"I don't buy it," Vicki said. "This is another trap you and Mrs. Jenness have cooked up, right?"

Coach Handlesman looked at Vicki. She wanted to believe him, but there were so many questions.

"You were against us from the start," Vicki said. "You took John's and Mark's Bibles."

"They got them back, didn't they?" Coach Handlesman said.

"You tried to get me to rat on my friends."

"I was trying to help you. If I got you to come clean before the GC authorities got involved, I thought I could protect you. But you kids kept it up."

"Mrs. Weems said somebody spoke up for me, got me into a foster family."

"Guilty," Coach Handlesman said. "Sometimes when you pretend to be someone else, you pretend really well. They believed every word."

"But I saw you at church! Yelling at Bruce."

"I saw you first and made it look good.

Bruce is my dearest friend now. I didn't want to endanger him or you, so I tried to make it look good."

"What about Mrs. Waltonen?"

The coach shrugged. "I took a chance. She was asking questions. She wondered about her grandchild. Said you had talked with her, tried to give her answers. I thought she was sincere. I told her God was behind the disappearances. Her granddaughter's in heaven now."

"How did she react?"

"She got quiet. I thought she might break, but then she came at me like a dog. She said if God could be so mean, she'd never believe."

"And she turned you in?"

"Not then. Shelly was excited to see you and told me to come outside. Waltonen must have followed and put it all together when she saw you."

"You told Shelly about us?" Vicki said.

"I could tell she was going to break if somebody didn't. I explained that I was just trying to help, and that she shouldn't blame herself for your being taken away. You were with a foster family, and things were going OK now."

Coach Handlesman took off his hat, and

Vicki saw the huge bruise on his head. "What happened?" she asked.

"That little slugger at Judd's house—what's his name? The kid with the dog?"

"Ryan?"

"Clocked me a good one with a golf club."

"What were you doing at the house?"

"Mrs. Jenness set a trap for Judd. She had Mrs. Weems send a message on that watch thing you guys have. Tried to trick them into coming to the school. I figured it was all over, so I went to Judd's house to hide the papers or whatever else might be there that would give you guys away."

"You would have destroyed the computer files?"

"No, I would have copied and hid 'em."

"So they still don't know whether Judd's guilty?"

"No hard proof."

"But if they catch him at the airport and take his files from home, he's sunk."

"Looks that way."

"Were you the one following me the other day?"

"Couldn't find you. Jenness called out the GC guards. They spotted you first."

"What about you? What happens now?"

He shrugged. "Fired. Suspended. Charged with something. I don't know."

Bruce and Judd hurried past the flight attendants as they went through their safety routines. They panted as they buckled their seat belts and settled in.

Mrs. Jenness and Superintendent Pembroke returned with grim faces.

"Thompson is gone," Mrs. Jenness said. "His plane left a few minutes ago."

Superintendent Pembroke looked sternly at Coach Handlesman. "I'm suspending you without pay. Clean out your office. We'll hold a hearing next week."

The principal pulled the others into the next room to confer. Coach Handlesman stopped her and nodded toward Vicki. "She ought to be free now, right?"

"Wrong," Mrs. Jenness said. "She's still a ward of the Global Community."

"If I go back to that place," Vicki said when she and the coach were alone again, "there's nobody to take care of Judd's files. I've got no way to reach the others."

The Mole

Just then Chaya pecked at the window and motioned to Vicki. Coach Handlesman opened it, and Vicki quickly climbed through.

"I'll cover for you," Coach Handlesman said as he closed the window behind her.

Chaya drove Vicki to New Hope Village Church, where they learned that Judd and Bruce would be in Israel for two weeks. Vicki had lost her family. Now the two people closest to her were half a world away, and she was on the run. The detention center was one thing. Being alone again made her shiver. At least she had Chaya.

NINE

The Trip

JUDD had not been on a plane since the disappearances. Both he and Bruce were tired, but each time one of them stretched to close his eyes, the other brought up a new topic, and they talked for hours. At one point Judd squirmed and cleared his throat.

"I was wondering what you thought about, uh, you know, dating and stuff."

"Dating and stuff?" Bruce said.

Judd felt his face flush. "Ryan calls it the mushy stuff. If we have only seven years left, should we forget about that kind of thing? I mean, wouldn't it take you away from doing what's important?"

Bruce smiled. "We've gone through this with the adult Trib Force with Chloe and Buck. Whether they get married or not is still open, but I do know they've been good for each other."

"But what about somebody my age?" Judd

said. "Chloe's in college. Buck is . . . well, he's ancient."

Bruce raised his eyebrows. "Try to find friends, good friends. Don't get entangled in a romance. Dating someone doesn't make you happy or fulfilled."

"I know. But sometimes . . ."

"I know. I miss my wife like nothing else. But God has a plan. Yearn for a deeper relationship with him."

Chaya didn't want to leave Vicki alone, especially in the dead of night, but Vicki insisted. The two hugged and promised to keep in touch.

Judd's house was dark. Vicki stole to the back and rang the doorbell. Phoenix didn't bark, so she knew Ryan and Lionel weren't there. She couldn't wait for help. She would have to do this alone.

Getting into Judd's house was not easy. The windows were high. The back door, Vicki knew, had double locks. Near the deck a small, oval window led into the garage. If she managed to get through it, the basement door was next. She hoped someone had left it unlocked.

Vicki picked up a rock and tapped on the glass. Too noisy. She found a rag on the picnic table and held it up to the glass, then drove the rock through it. She stopped and listened. A dog barked nearby, then silence. One by one she picked out the remaining shards and carefully placed them aside. The hole would be just big enough for her to slip through.

A taxi let jet-lagged Judd and Bruce out near some tour buses. The two gathered their carry-on bags and hustled into the early morning crowd spilling into the street. They pressed forward but were only able to get about a hundred yards from the two witnesses.

Eli and Moishe used no amplification, but their voices rang clearly off the ancient walls.

"The last terrible week of the Lord has begun!" Eli bellowed. "Israel has turned from the true Messiah!"

Moishe took up the strain. "Israel is even now rebuilding the temple. It is a temple of rejection!"

A man in the crowd yelled, "Mercy!" and fell to the ground. Those nearby shushed him, but the more they did, the more the man wept and cried out.

Judd pointed toward the Wailing Wall. Eli and Moishe moved away from their perch and walked directly toward Bruce and Judd.

The crowd parted, and Judd thought of Moses and the Red Sea. Eli and Moishe came to the place where the man lay prostrate and moaning. They wore ragged robes. Their arms were muscled and leathery. They had huge, bony hands and wore no shoes. The scent of ashes, as if from a recent fire, hung about them.

"To the one who seeks mercy, mercy will be given," Eli said. "But only one is merciful."

"The Lord God is rich in mercy," Moishe said. "He loved you so much that even while you were dead in your sins, he gave you life when he raised Christ from the dead."

The man cried out again, "Forgive me! I have rejected the holy one of God! Forgive me!"

Others fell to their knees and cried out. Judd heard someone speaking in Spanish, another in what sounded like German, and still others in languages he had never heard before.

"God's blessing upon you," Moishe said as he placed his hand on the man. "May you know the peace of Jesus Christ and the presence of the Holy Spirit. Amen."

Judd's knees went weak as the men backed away. He was speechless.

"Come with me," Bruce whispered. Judd followed him across the road to a small grove of trees.

Bruce spoke through tears. "It's beginning. The Jews, who have so long rejected Jesus as Messiah, are returning. It's as if we're on holy ground."

He motioned for Judd to follow while he hailed a cab. He gave the driver an address on a scrap of paper.

Vicki wrapped her bleeding leg with a fresh bandage from upstairs. She hadn't seen the piece of glass that cut so deeply. *I've gotta help Judd,* was her only thought.

She gathered paper and supplies and put them in a garbage bag. Then she unscrewed the computer connections. She left the printers, monitors, and other equipment and moved the computer towers to the garage.

Shelly! she thought. *If Handlesman was right, Shelly would surely help.*

Bruce rang the doorbell of a modest Israeli home. The door opened slightly, and a middle-aged woman looked at them warily.

"I was looking for the house of the rabbi," Bruce said.

"Why?"

"I . . . I am a follower of Christ," Bruce said.

Judd turned as a black car passed slowly behind them.

The woman grabbed Bruce's arm. "Come in. Quickly!"

Bruce and Judd stepped inside.

"It is not safe for you here," she said.

"I'm not worried," Bruce said. "God is protecting us."

"You sound like my husband."

"Is he here?"

"Who are you? Where are you from?"

"Bruce Barnes. I'm a pastor from America."

"If you are a pastor, why were you left behind?"

Bruce quickly told her his story.

"How do I know I can trust you?" she said.

"A mutual friend gave me your address—Buck Williams, the writer."

Relief came over the woman's face. "Eli and Moishe have asked my husband to speak at Teddy Kollek Stadium," she said. "It is an honor he says he does not deserve. It is an honor I would like someone else's husband to have."

She handed Bruce a piece of paper and told him to take it to the stadium that evening. "You must be discreet," she said. "We believe anyone who goes in or out of our home is in danger."

Judd heard another car pass slowly and peeked through the curtains.

"Stay away from the front window," she said. "Why don't you join my children in the kitchen?"

Fresh bread was on the table. A boy about Judd's age sat there. He wore glasses and had close-cropped black hair. A girl who looked slightly older stood by the stove with her arms crossed. She nodded gravely to Judd.

"American?" she said.

"From Chicago. I'm Judd Thompson."

The girl introduced herself as Nina Ben-Judah and the boy as her brother, Dan.

"The rabbi is your father?" Judd said.

"Stepfather," she said. "Our father died when we were young."

"Is your mom always like this?" Judd said. "She seems really nervous."

"My father's life has been threatened," Dan said. "He is trying to arrange for armed guards."

"Just because of what he said on TV?"

Nina said, "Of course! That was blasphemy here. Many believed his message and have become followers, but most think he is a traitor to his faith."

"What about you?" Judd asked her.

She looked at him, squinting. "You first," she said. "Are you a Christian?"

"Yes, I am."

Nina looked at Dan and smiled. "We are

not ashamed of the gospel of Christ," she said. "It is the power of God to salvation for everyone who believes, for the Jew first and also for the Greek."

Judd recognized the verse she quoted. "When?" he said. "How?"

"Our father told us of his study," Dan said. "He nearly became a believer before the Rapture."

"We now know our Messiah," Nina said, "but we have become prisoners in our own home. We have to sneak out to go anywhere. Would you like to see the old city?"

Judd told Bruce he would meet him that evening at Teddy Kollek Stadium.

"Why? Where are you going?"

Judd nodded toward Nina.

"No!" her mother said. "Nina, please! It is too dangerous."

"Mother! Trust me! We have an American guest."

Nina led Judd to a trapdoor under a rug in the kitchen. A small passageway led next door where neighbors hustled Nina, Judd, and Dan out a back entrance and into a car. Nina jumped behind the wheel and sped off.

"Do you have to go through there every time you leave?" Judd said.

Dan nodded. "We must not be seen."

The kids knew Hebrew custom and history

well. Judd was amazed to think that Jesus actually walked these same roads, carried the cross, was crucified, and rose again in this ancient land. He was awestruck at the Garden of Gethsemane. That afternoon the Bible came alive to him.

By the end of the day Judd felt a bond with Nina and Dan he couldn't explain. He had known them less than a day, yet they were his brother and sister in Christ. As evening approached they stopped at a café. Halfway through the meal, Dan said something in Hebrew, and Nina furtively looked toward the street.

"Kollek Stadium is less than a kilometer away," she said. "There is an exit near the rest rooms in the back. Go there now. When you are outside again, follow that street. You'll make it in plenty of time."

"What are you going to do?" Judd said.

Nina kissed Judd on one cheek and then the other. He saw her tears.

"God bless you and keep you, my brother," she said, "and cause his face to shine upon you."

Judd disappeared inside the café, hoping Nina and Dan would be all right.

Teddy Kollek Stadium was filled. Judd felt both fear and excitement as Eli and Moishe spoke without an interpreter to people from around the world.

"You have been gathered from the twelve tribes of Israel, the chosen ones of the Almighty. And we have been given the high calling of proclaiming his name to every nation, every tribe, every tongue—

"We do not trust in numbers," Moishe picked up the message. "We do not trust in the power of persuasive speech. We trust in the name of the Lord, our God!"

A shout of affirmation shook the stadium.

"One day very soon," Eli said, "every knee shall bow and every tongue confess that Jesus Christ is Lord."

". . . to the glory of God, the Father," Moishe said.

"To the glory of God," they said in unison. And then the multitude, in one voice, thundered the response, "TO THE GLORY OF GOD!!!"

Eli introduced Rabbi Tsion Ben-Judah. He was middle-aged, trim, and youthful-looking, with only a hint of gray in his dark brown hair. He wore a black suit.

"Dear ones," Ben-Judah said. "How I praise God for each of you. Throughout history we have been a scattered people. Now God is calling us together to be his vessels of reconciliation. He has chosen us

to proclaim freedom to the captives! All
praise and glory to the Most High God!"

Judd made his way to a glassed-in booth
high in the stadium, where he looked over
Bruce's shoulder as he tapped out an E-mail
message to the adult Tribulation Force.

As I look into this sea of faces, he wrote, *from
every conceivable background, I am moved as
never before. God's Word is true. Before my very
eyes I see God's plan to carry the gospel to the
ends of the earth. But my friends, be warned.
Though the message is being accepted like never
before, though there is coming an incredible soul
harvest, there is also coming great trouble.
Antichrist is preparing an assault on believers.
The question is how long we have.*

Vicki called Shelly, and she agreed to help.
They would take the computers to Shelly's
trailer or the church. Anywhere but Judd's
house. Vicki heard a car in the driveway and
hit the button for the automatic door. Vicki
shielded her eyes from the flashing red and
blue lights.

A voice boomed, "This is the police. Put
your hands up and move away from the
house!"

TEN

A Favor Returned

OF ALL the sights in Israel, the most amazing and frightening to Judd was the new temple. It looked magnificent. Many said it surpassed the glory of Solomon's temple of old. Judd knew this temple was not built to praise God but rather his enemy.

That evening, as Judd downloaded a day's worth of E-mail, Bruce told him he had met a man from Singapore at the stadium the night before. "He invited us to hold meetings next week in the same stadium Dr. Ben-Judah will use next month when he's there. God is answering our prayers."

"Fantastic!" Judd said. He opened an urgent message from John. Judd slumped. "Vicki's in trouble again—this time with the police."

"Police?" Bruce said.

"John also says Coach Handlesman has been detained. What in the world—?"

Bruce told Judd the truth about Coach Handlesman. Coach had prayed to receive Christ in Bruce's office, and Bruce encouraged him to take his new faith back to school. "He's been worried about you kids for so long. We'll need to get back right away and help him."

"Wait," Judd said. "If God wants you in Singapore, that's where you should go."

"I wouldn't want to abandon Vicki or Coach Handlesman when they need me most," Bruce said.

"You're not abandoning them," Judd said. "They would want you to follow God's leading. I'll go back."

Bruce shook his head, but Judd pressed. "You've said yourself that we were left here to reach those who don't know God. This is a great opportunity for you. I can handle this."

"I hate to send you back alone."

"I'll be fine. This feels right, Bruce."

"If you're sure . . ."

"I'm sure."

Vicki had tripped a silent alarm when she climbed through the window. As Vicki was led to the police cruiser, Shelly passed by. "Go home," Vicki mouthed.

Shelly nodded and kept moving.

The big problem now was the evidence. If Global Community goons found the computer files, Judd would be toast.

At the police station, Vicki was allowed one call.

An hour later a guard approached her. "There's someone to see you." She led Vicki through a packed waiting room and into a private holding area. Vicki brightened when she saw Chaya.

"Hiya, sis," Vicki said, cautious with a guard nearby.

"I'm glad you called me. I want to help, but I don't know how. Do you need a lawyer or something?"

"I think I have it figured out," Vicki said, bending to whisper to Chaya.

"No whispering," the guard said.

Chaya sat back. "I can do that."

"Good," Vicki said. She wrote a phone number on a piece of paper. "Call my friend Shelly, too. She'll be worried. Now, what about you? I've been thinking. You're all alone, and you want to learn more about the Bible."

"Exactly," Chaya said.

"Move here," Vicki said. "Get an apartment

near the church. Bruce is the best teacher of the Scriptures."

The guard answered a knock at the door and stepped outside.

"It's tempting," Chaya said. "I'd have to get another job. . . ."

Chaya suddenly put a hand to her mouth. Vicki turned and saw Mrs. Weems and the Steins.

Chaya looked at her parents. Her father turned away, but her mother seemed to lock eyes with her. When Mrs. Weems led the Steins from the room, Chaya wept.

Judd found an empty row on the plane and stretched out. Leaving Bruce was hard, but he knew it was right.

At the airport Bruce had slipped a piece of paper into Judd's pocket. Judd opened it and read:

"To Judd, my son in the faith. Words can't express how much you have meant on this trip, and I will always remember your service. I hope we can one day finish a trip together.

"Hold fast to the hope you have in Christ. Fight the good fight of faith, lay hold on eternal life, to which you were also called and have confessed the good confession in the presence of many witnesses.

"If those words seem familiar, they are Paul's instructions to Timothy. Read 1 and 2 Timothy on your way home. Tell Vicki and Mr. Handlesman they are in my prayers. I remember Lionel and Ryan daily as well.

"May God's grace be with you all. Bruce."

Judd read the passages and was struck especially by 2 Timothy 3:12: "Yes, and all who desire to live godly in Christ Jesus will suffer persecution."

Finally back in Chicago, a customs officer took Judd's passport and ushered him into a waiting room.

Two hours later Judd was fuming. He banged on the door.

"What's this about?" he yelled. "I didn't bring anything back but clothes."

Finally, a tall, thin man entered. He was balding, and Judd couldn't help staring at the wrinkles in his forehead. He pulled a chair across the room close to Judd. He extended a hand, which Judd shook reluctantly.

"Stan Barkoczyk, Global Community task force. Your name came up in an investigation we're pursuing. How well do you know Mr. Handlesman?"

"Not well," Judd said.

"He hasn't helped you?"

"Helped me what? Do more chin-ups in gym? Run the mile a little faster?"

"You're a religious type, aren't you?"

"Depends on how you define *religious.*"

Barkoczyk leaned toward Judd, inches from his face. Judd smelled his stale breath. Foamy beads of white formed at the corners of his mouth. "I define *religious* as undermining the Global Community. Religious types think they know more than everybody else and can't wait to show how stupid they are."

Mr. Barkoczyk leaned back and crossed his legs. Judd locked eyes with him and remained silent.

Later Mr. Barkoczyk drove Judd to a police station. Principal Jenness and Superintendent Pembroke shook hands with Mr. Barkoczyk, and the four were led into a cluttered evidence room. Judd's computers sat on a table in the middle of the room.

"Would you like to show us, or do we have to find it ourselves?" Mr. Barkoczyk said.

Judd knew they had him. When they opened his computer files, he would have to tell them everything.

Mrs. Weems led Vicki to the infirmary, where a nurse changed the bandage on her leg.

"I didn't have a chance to apologize about your little message machine," Mrs. Weems said. "And it looks like your boyfriend is back. He'll get his today."

"Don't bet on it," Vicki muttered. "And he's not my boyfriend."

The girls hooted when Vicki returned. "Preacher girl is back!" one girl said. "The one who got Janie in trouble."

"Where is Janie?" Vicki said.

"What's it to you?" the girl said. "She's been in the hole since the day you got sprung."

That night, Mrs. Weems showed what she called a "motivational film." It was a Global Community production targeted to troubled teens. While the girls groused about the subject, it was one of the few times they were allowed to watch TV.

The face of Nicolae Carpathia appeared on the screen.

"He's pretty cute," one girl said.

While the narrator extolled the virtues of peace and harmony, Vicki fell to her knees and crept to the back of the room. She opened the door silently and sneaked into the solitary confinement area. She tried several rooms in the dim light of the hallway. Finally, she opened a slat and saw two hollow eyes.

Vicki pushed an apple through the hole. "It's not much, but it's the least I could do after what you did for me."

"What're you doing back in?"

"Long story," Vicki said. "You OK? Can I get you anything else?"

"As soon as it's safe," Janie said, "come back and talk? I'm going crazy in here."

Judd turned on the first computer as the others inched closer. His mind raced. *Could he delete the files? Not with them watching.* Mr. Barkoczyk leaned over Judd's shoulder as the screen flickered. "System error" was all Judd could see.

"What is it?" Barkoczyk said.

"I don't know," Judd said.

Mr. Barkoczyk turned crimson and shoved Judd out of the way. He banged the keyboard and switched the computers off and on. The screens were blank. A computer technician was called in.

"Both dead, sir," the man concluded.

"Hard drives crashed. Not a thing I can do for you."

Mr. Barkoczyk cursed and marched a relieved but puzzled Judd past the front desk and told him to wait in the lobby.

A few chairs away an officer put down his newspaper.

"Hello, Judd," he said.

Judd couldn't believe his eyes. Sergeant Tom Fogarty.

"Just be calm," Sergeant Fogarty said. "Don't act like you know me."

"How did you know I was here?" Judd whispered.

"I've been keeping an eye on some of the Global Community reports. Vicki's friend Chaya called and asked for help. When I heard the GC was involved, I thought I'd better check it out."

"What did you do?"

Sergeant Fogarty smiled. "I took a look at your computers. I never was much good with those things. I'm afraid I may have messed up your hard drives. Hope you don't mind."

Judd sighed. "Thanks. So what happens to me now?"

"I can't imagine. They have no evidence."

Sergeant Fogarty lifted his newspaper as Mr. Barkoczyk and the others returned.

Mrs. Jenness and Mr. Pembroke stared at the floor. "You're free to go, Thompson. But I'd watch my step if I were you."

Judd walked into the fading sunlight with a carton of damaged computer equipment. He would face difficult decisions soon. What about the *Underground*? What about staying in his home? Judd's senior year was approaching. What then? College seemed out of the question. Or was it? Could he rescue Vicki or even get a message to her? It felt like a lifetime since Judd had spoken to her.

Lionel and Ryan kept Judd up late, bringing him up to date and asking about his trip to Israel. They wanted to know every detail about Israel and Judd's new friends there. Judd flipped through a stack of mail as he talked. He slipped one envelope into his pocket and put the rest aside.

Before he went to sleep he retrieved an old laptop from his father's desk to go on-line. Only one E-mail interested him. It was from Bruce.

"God is at work," Judd read, "raising up house churches and small groups. The day is coming when such will be outlawed. I hope you are safe, Judd. I pray for you each day."

Judd was glad to be in his own bed, but the envelope in his pocket kept him from sleep. He couldn't tell anyone. It was a bank statement. His father's account, which he thought would easily last the next seven years, was dangerously low. They would be lucky if the money lasted seven months.

ABOUT THE AUTHORS

Jerry B. Jenkins (www.jerryjenkins.com) is the writer of the Left Behind series. He is author of more than one hundred books, of which six have reached the *New York Times* best-seller list. Former vice president for publishing for the Moody Bible Institute of Chicago, he also served many years as editor of *Moody* magazine and is now Moody's writer-at-large.

His writing has appeared in publications as varied as *Reader's Digest, Parade*, in-flight magazines, and many Christian periodicals. He has written books in four genres: biography, marriage and family, fiction for children, and fiction for adults.

Jenkins's biographies include books with Hank Aaron, Bill Gaither, Luis Palau, Walter Payton, Orel Hershiser, Nolan Ryan, Brett Butler, and Billy Graham, among many others.

Six of his apocalyptic novels—*Left Behind, Tribulation Force, Nicolae, Soul Harvest, Apollyon*, and *Assassins*—have appeared on the Christian Booksellers Association's best-selling fiction list and the *Publishers Weekly* religion best-seller list. *Left Behind* was nominated for Book of the Year by the Evangelical Christian Publishers Association in 1997, 1998, and 1999.

As a marriage and family author and speaker, Jenkins has been a frequent guest on Dr. James Dobson's *Focus on the Family* radio program.

Jerry is also the writer of the nationally syndicated sports story comic strip *Gil Thorp*, distributed to newspapers across the United States by Tribune Media Services.

Jerry and his wife, Dianna, live in Colorado.

Limited speaking engagement information available through speaking@jerryjenkins.com.

Dr. Tim LaHaye (www.timlahayeministries.org), who conceived the idea of fictionalizing an account of the Rapture and the Tribulation, is a noted author, minister, educator, and nationally recognized speaker on Bible prophecy. He presides over Tim LaHaye Ministries and is chairman and founder of the Pre-Trib Research Center. Presently Dr. LaHaye speaks at many of the major Bible prophecy conferences in the U.S. and Canada, where his eight current prophecy books are very popular.

Dr. LaHaye is a graduate of Bob Jones University and holds the D.Min. from Western Theological Seminary and the Lit.D. from Liberty University. For twenty-five years he pastored one of the nation's outstanding churches in San Diego, which grew to three locations. It was during that time that he founded two accredited Christian high schools, a Christian school system of ten schools, and Christian Heritage College.

Dr. LaHaye has written over forty books, with over 22 million copies in print in thirty-two languages. He has written books on a wide variety of subjects, such as family life, temperaments, and Bible prophecy. His current fiction works, written by Jerry Jenkins—*Left Behind, Tribulation Force, Nicolae, Soul Harvest, Apollyon,* and *Assassins*—have all reached number one on the Christian best-seller charts. Other works by Dr. LaHaye are *Spirit-Controlled Temperament; How to Be Happy though Married; The Act of Marriage; Revelation Unveiled; Understanding the Last Days; Rapture under Attack: Will You Escape the Tribulation?; Are We Living in the End Times?;* and the youth fiction series Left Behind: The Kids.

He is the father of four children and grandfather of nine. Snow skiing, waterskiing, motorcycling, golfing, vacationing with family, and jogging are among his leisure activities.